Usborne

Sparkly Princesses Sticker Book

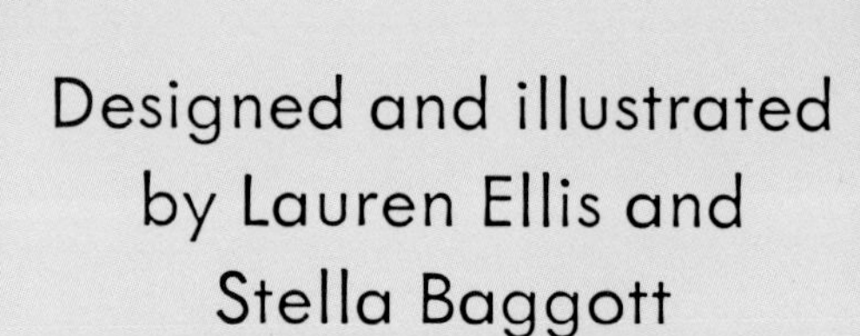

Designed and illustrated by Lauren Ellis and Stella Baggott

Words by Kirsteen Robson

Additional design by Winsome d'Abreu

You'll find all the stickers at the back of the book.

The princesses enjoy rides out in their golden carriage...

...pulled along by their faithful pony, Flapjack.

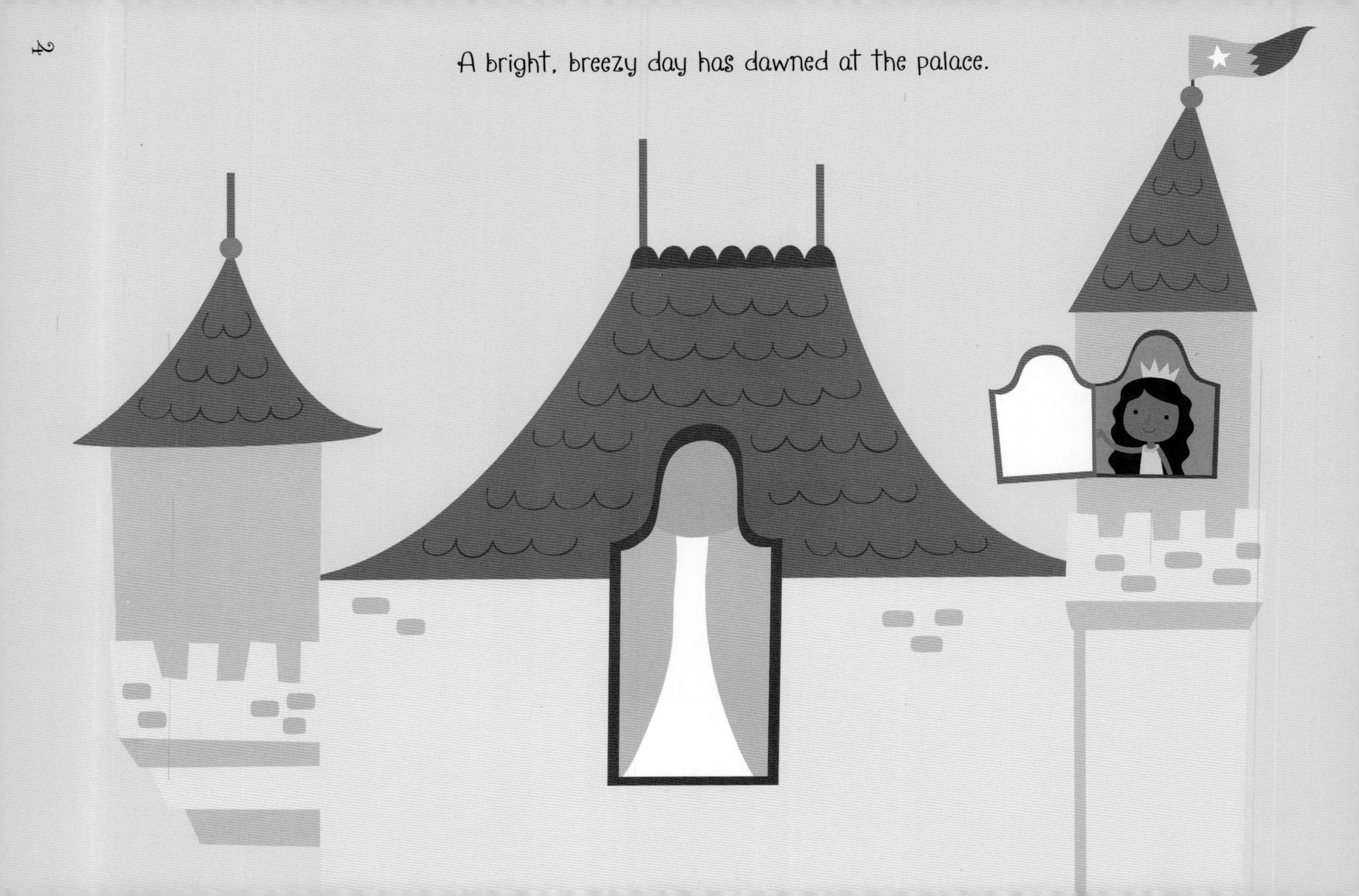

A bright, breezy day has dawned at the palace.

The princesses are always up early,
and as busy as bees.

At the fair the princesses love watching the archery contests.

They are looking forward to the ladies' competition, where they can show off their skills with a bow and arrow.

The treasury is full of jewels that have been in the royal family for hundreds of years.

It's never too early for a mouthful of coffee and cake. Mmmmm...!

On crisp, icy winter days, the princesses have fun gliding around on the frozen lake.

The princesses love to walk through the meadows...

...enjoying the fresh air and sunshine.

Merry music fills the air and the princesses are ready to dance at the masked ball.

Guided by moonlight and starlight, the princesses like to visit their forest friends.